E KATS J
Kats, Jewel, 1978-2016.
Snow White's seven patches : a
vitiligo fairy tale

Snow White's Seven Patches:

A Vitiligo Fairy Tale

✳✳✳

Story by Jewel Kats

Illustrated by Dan Goodfellow

From the Fairy Ability Tales Series
LOVING HEALING PRESS

Snow White's Seven Patches: A Vitiligo Fairy Tale
Copyright (c) 2013 by Jewel Kats. All Rights Reserved
Illustrated by Dan Goodfellow
Book #3 in the Fairy Ability Tales Series

Library of Congress Cataloging-in-Publication Data
Kats, Jewel, 1978-
Snow White's seven patches : a vitiligo fairy tale / story by Jewel Kats ; illustrated by Dan Goodfellow.
pages cm. -- (Fairy ability tales)
Summary: Beautiful but vain Ivy locks away her infant daughter, Snow, because she is born with a skin disorder, and later forces her to write children's books until Snow escapes and finds shelter in the forest , in this story based on the Grimm fairy tale.
ISBN 978-1-61599-206-5 (pbk. : alk. paper) -- ISBN 978-1-61599-207-2 (hardcover : alk. paper) -- ISBN 978-1-61599-208-9 (ebook)
[1. Self-realization--Fiction. 2. Vitiligo--Fiction.. 3. Beauty, Personal--Fiction. 4. Pride and vanity--Fiction. 5. Mothers and daughters--Fiction.] I. Goodfellow, Dan, illustrator. II. Title.
PZ7.K157445Sno 2014
[E]--dc23
2013036159

Learn more at www.JewelKats.com

Published by:
Loving Healing Press
5145 Pontiac Trail
Ann Arbor, MI 48105

www.LHPress.com
info@LHPress.com
Tollfree (USA/CAN) 888-761-6268
Fax 734-663-6861

Distributed by: Ingram Book Group (USA/CAN), New Leaf Distributing (USA), Bertram's Books (UK), Agapea (SP), Hachette Livre (FR)

The Fairy Ability Tales Series
1. Cinderella's Magical Wheelchair: An Empowering Fairy Tale
2. The Princess and the Ruby: An Autism Fairy Tale
3. Snow White's Seven Patches: A Vitiligo Fairy Tale

For every child kissed by beautiful puffs of white, thanks to the Fairies of Vitiligo

There once lived a very rich lady named Ivy. She thought the world of her own looks. Her beauty pageant crowns only added to her arrogance. Ivy made outrageous demands on her magic mirror once she became pregnant.

"Mirror, mirror on the wall, who's the finest-looking woman of all?" she'd ask.

"Why you!" the mirror would respond.

"Good," Ivy would answer. "Now, grant me a gorgeous child."

After nine months, it came time to deliver the baby. Ivy hired a big name doctor to help. With one last push, a wailing baby was born.

"Your girl has all ten fingers and toes," the doctor said.

"Who cares?!" Ivy huffed. "Is she *beautiful*?"

He wiped the newborn with a towel. "She has ebony hair, a cupid's mouth, and..." his voice trailed off, "seven white patches of skin. I'm afraid she has a condition called vitiligo."

"*WHAT?!!!*" Ivy roared.

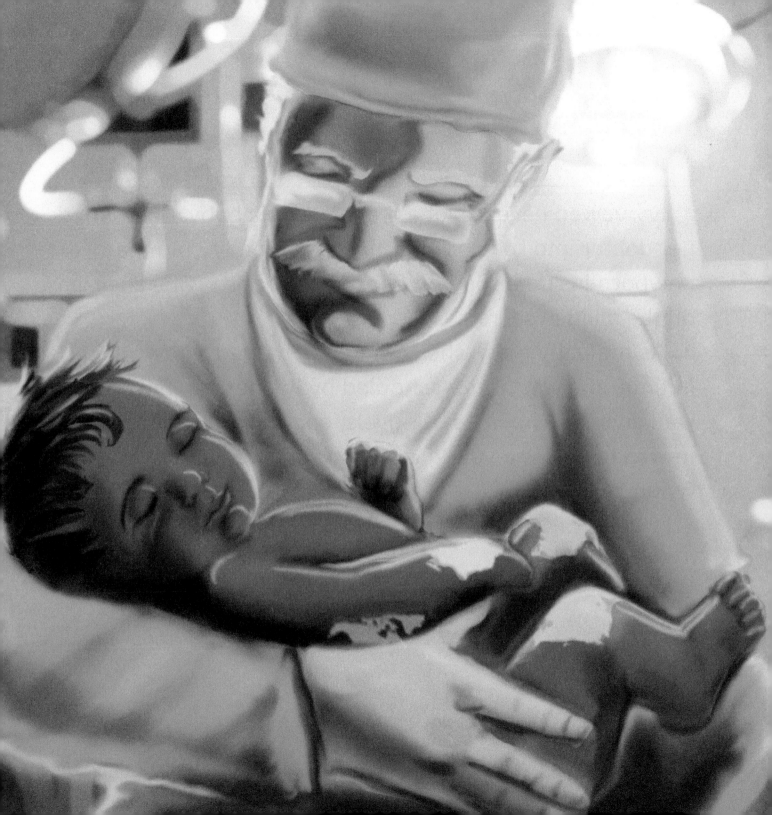

Ivy vowed never to let anyone see this baby. She bribed her doctor into keeping this birth a secret. Ivy hid the newborn inside a shed on her huge property. She checked on the child in secret.

As the baby grew, she came to be named Snow White. In time, she was home-schooled by Ivy herself. Snow was given the luxuries of novels, encyclopedias, and newspapers. As a young adult, she showed a flare for writing.

Locked in the shed, Snow was forced to write day and night like a machine. She never had a say over what she had to pen.

"You want me to write *another* children's book?" she asked. "For once, I wish I could write a love story…"

"Don't even think about it!" Ivy snapped. "You're lucky that I've kept you alive, and well. The least you can be is obedient."

Snow's head hung low.

Ivy tapped her high-heeled foot. "Now, have you finished the latest children's book?"

Snow handed over her work.

Ivy smirked. "Marvellous." She pulled an apple out from her pocket. "Here's your usual reward."

Snow bit into the apple hungrily. "Thank you."

Several weeks later, Ivy had come into the shed with the daily newspaper and a bulging sack.

"I'm going away," she announced. "I've brought you enough juice boxes, canned sardines, and biscuits to last you three weeks."

"Where are you traveling to?" Snow asked.

"You weren't given geography lessons for a reason," Ivy replied. "Your world is limited to this shed. Accept it."

"Is my life's only purpose to write about make-believe places?" Snow questioned.

"Yes," Ivy answered. "I expect another completed book upon my return. No ifs, ands, or buts about it."

Snow read the newspaper after Ivy left. However, her jaw dropped when she got to the back page. The newspaper had printed a dolled-up picture of Ivy. Snow was dumbfounded by the newspaper headline.

"*Award-Winning Children's Author Travels Seven Continents for Book Tour.*"

None of the books named in the article were written by Ivy. They were all created by Snow!

Snow was determined to learn more about the seven continents. She reached for an encyclopedia. That section of the book was taped shut. She ripped it open. Oddly, the shapes of the continents on the world map seemed familiar. Everything clicked the moment her eyes gazed at the white patches on her elbows.

"My seven patches are in the shape of the seven continents!" Snow whispered, touching the images on her hands, elbows, throat, and knees.

For the next few weeks, she daydreamed about the world.

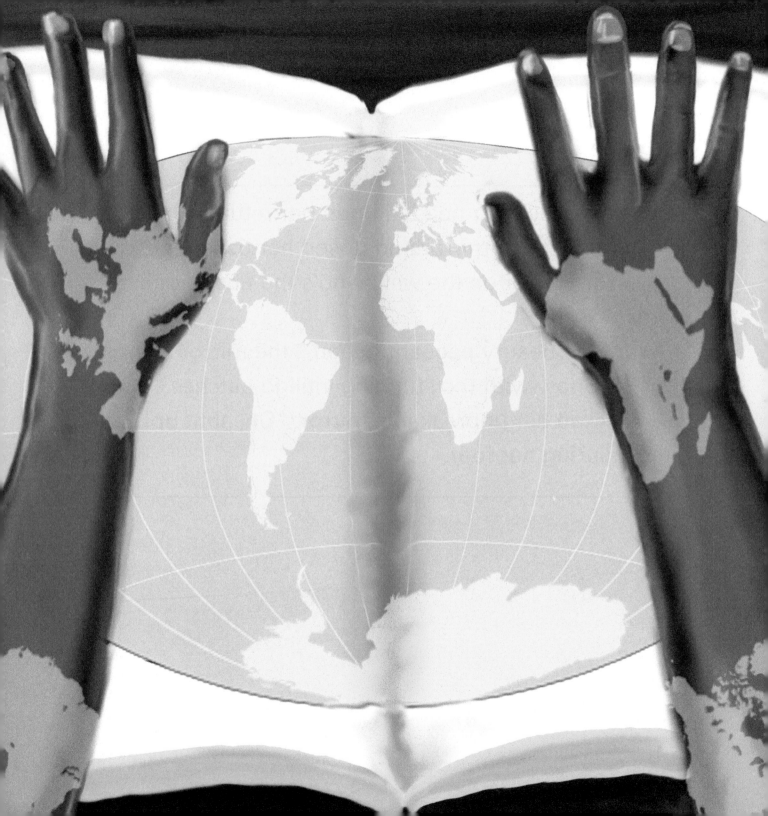

Ivy was really big-headed upon her return. She stood in front of her magic mirror and posed her usual question.

"Mirror, mirror on the wall, who's the finest-looking woman of all?"

"You're a beauty pageant queen," the mirror answered, "but it's Snow with the stunning vitiligo patches."

Ivy kicked her unbreakable mirror. "Oh, shut up!" she cried, injuring her foot.

Ivy limped to the shed and swung the door open.

"Hand over the stories you've written at once!" she commanded.

"I won't let you steal my work anymore," Snow answered.

Ivy grabbed a lit candle. "What good are you now?!" She began to chase after her. "Your patches started this mess in the first place. I'll burn them all off!"

Snow tore through the doorway and fled into the deep forest.

With a pounding heart, Snow only stopped running when she spotted a waterfall. A strong man stood washing his horse. She blinked. Snow decided to climb a tree to get a better look.

"I'd have better footing if it weren't for these rundown shoes—"

Right then, the branch broke. Her bottom fell straight to the ground!

The man at the waterfall caught sight. "Hey, Miss, are you all right?" he called.

Not looking back, Snow ran off with a red face.

Snow searched and searched for shelter. At long last, she stumbled upon a miniature house. She knocked at the petite gate. Nobody answered. She let herself inside. Snow was greeted by cobwebs and dirty plates. She wondered who lived there. Exhausted, she headed upstairs and hopped into a wee bed. She dreamt of the man and horse at the waterfall.

"Who are you?" a pipsqueak voice demanded.

Snow jolted awake. She had a family of three dwarfs breathing down her neck.

The largest of the dwarfs stepped forward. He tugged at his long beard. "I repeat: Who are you?"

Snow gulped. "I can explain!"

"You better start talking," their little boy said. "Papa doesn't like to wait."

Snow took a deep breath. She let out her whole story.

"You poor thing," Mama sighed. "You're welcome to stay with us."

"In exchange," Papa added, "you're expected to keep house."

Snow smiled. "You got it."

Snow cooked, cleaned, and wrote in her spare time. She penned a love story about the man at the waterfall. She'd been thinking about him ever since. On paper, she could at least pretend he loved her. In real life, Snow dared not think that. On the day the novel was finally done, there was a knock at the door.

"Would you like to buy some apples?" a strangely familiar old woman asked.

"You have perfect timing!" Snow exclaimed. "I can bake a pie to celebrate with my friends."

The old woman handed over an apple. "Let me treat you right now."

Snow took a bite and collapsed to the floor.

The old woman took off her cloak to reveal her real identity as Ivy. "Now, it's my turn to celebrate!"

Forest doctors were unable to wake up Snow. The dwarf family placed her in a crystal casket alongside her finished novel. One day, the man from the waterfall came to see the famed resting woman.

He got down on his knees at the sight of her. "My goodness, it's you!" Charles said, stroking Snow's cheek. "I've thought of you every day since I saw you fall from that tree." He reached into her casket and pulled out her book.

Charles paced back-and-forth while reading. He smiled and returned to her side. "This love story tells me you never forgot about me either." He felt his heart pull. "I wish I'd had the chance to talk with you...or hear you giggle...."

Snow continued to sleep silently.

He held her hands. "Even resting, I think you're the most beautiful woman on the planet." One by one, he kissed all seven of Snow's vitiligo patches.

Magically, she stirred awake.

Eventually, Snow and her dream man, Charles, married. They travelled to all seven continents on their honeymoon. Snow's book not only got published, but became a bestseller. As for Ivy, she got sued, and spent her time in a mirror-less jail cell.

The End

Just Married

About the Author

Once a teen runaway, Jewel Kats is now a two-time Mom's Choice Award winner. For six years, Jewel penned a syndicated teen advice column for Scripps Howard News Service (USA) and *The Halifax Chronicle Herald*. She gained this position through The Young People's Press. She's won $20,000 in scholarships from Global Television Network, and women's book publisher: Harlequin Enterprises. Jewel also interned in the TV studio of *Entertainment Tonight Canada*. Her books have been featured in *Ability Magazine* (USA) twice. She's authored eight books. Jewel is the writer, and real-life character behind *DitzAbled Princess*—a popular reality-series comic strip.

Please visit Jewel: www.jewelkats.com

About the Illustrator

Dan Goodfellow's illustration career has included painting backdrops for theatrical productions, album covers, instructional diagrams, comic books, faeries and mythological creatures, animation and, of course, children's books. On the rare occasions that he isn't holding a pencil, he can be found playing his drum on the top of Glastonbury Tor. He lives with his family in Somerset, UK.

Please visit Dan at www.dangoodfellow.co.uk

Also by Jewel Kats

**Cinderella's Magical Wheelchair:
An Empowering Fairy Tale**

**What Do You Use to Help Your Body?
Maggie Explores the World of Disabilities**

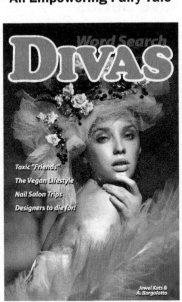

Word Search Divas

**Reena's Bollywood Dream:
A Story about Sexual Abuse**

www.JewelKats.com

Also by Jewel Kats

**Teddy Bear Princess:
A Story about Sharing and Caring**

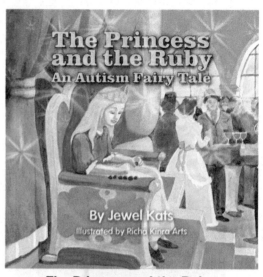

**The Princess and the Ruby:
An Autism Fairy Tale**

From the Growing with Love Series

**Billy Had to Move:
A Foster Care Story**

**Please Explain "Anxiety" to Me!
Simple Biology & Solutiosn for Children**

www.LHPress.com/growing-with-love

From the Growing with Love Series

I'm Not Weird, I Have SPD

Ferdinand Uses the Potty

www.LHPress.com/growing-with-love

CPSIA information can be obtained
at www.ICGtesting.com
Printed in the USA
BVOW07*0735180117

473509BV00011B/2/P